Parents and Caregivers,

Stone Arch Readers are designed to provide enjoyable reading experiences, as well as opportunities to develop vocabulary, literacy skills, and comprehension. Here are a few ways to support your beginning reader:

- Talk with your child about the ideas addressed in the story.

- Discuss each illustration, mentioning the characters, where they are, and what they are doing.

- Read with expression, pointing to each word. You may want to read the whole story through and then revisit parts of the story to ensure that the meanings of words or phrases are understood.

- Talk about why the character did what he or she did and what your child would do in that situation.

- Help your child connect with characters and events in the story.

Remember, reading with your child should be fun, not forced. Each moment spent reading with your child is a priceless investment in his or her literacy life.

Gail Saunders-Smith, Ph.D.

STONE ARCH **READERS**

are published by Stone Arch Books, a Capstone Imprint
151 Good Counsel Drive, P.O. Box 669
Mankato, Minnesota 56002
www.capstonepub.com

Library of Congress Cataloging-in-Publication data
is available on the Library of Congress website.
ISBN: 978-1-4342-2513-9 (library binding)
ISBN: 978-1-4342-3053-9 (paperback)

Summary: Andy is having a Halloween party for the Pet Club. However, he
doesn't know what kind of costume to make for his pet fish, Nibbles.

Reading Consultants:
Gail Saunders-Smith, Ph.D.
Melinda Melton Crow, M.Ed.
Laurie K. Holland, Media Specialist

Art Director: Kay Fraser
Designer: Emily Harris
Production Specialist: Michelle Biedscheid

Printed in the United States of America in Stevens Point, Wisconsin.
092010
005934WZS11

Pet Costume Party

A **PET CLUB** STORY

by Gwendolyn Hooks

illustrated by Mike Byrne

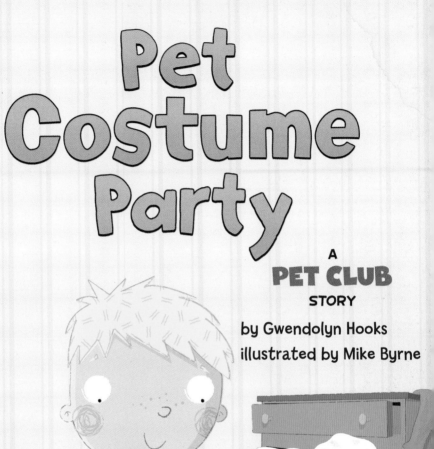

STONE ARCH BOOKS
a capstone imprint

Meet the PET CLUB!

Lucy
Jake
Buddy
Ajax

Lucy, Jake, Kayla, and Andy are best friends. Lucy has a rat named Ajax. Jake has a dog named Buddy.

Kayla

Andy

Daisy

Nibbles

Kayla has a cat named Daisy.
Andy has a fish named Nibbles.
Together, they are the Pet Club!

"It's Halloween. Let's have a
party tonight! Everyone can
dress up," Andy says.

Nibbles is excited.

Andy calls the Pet Club. Everyone can come.

"This is going to be so fun!"
Andy says.

"What should we dress up like?
I've never seen a costume for a
fish," he says.

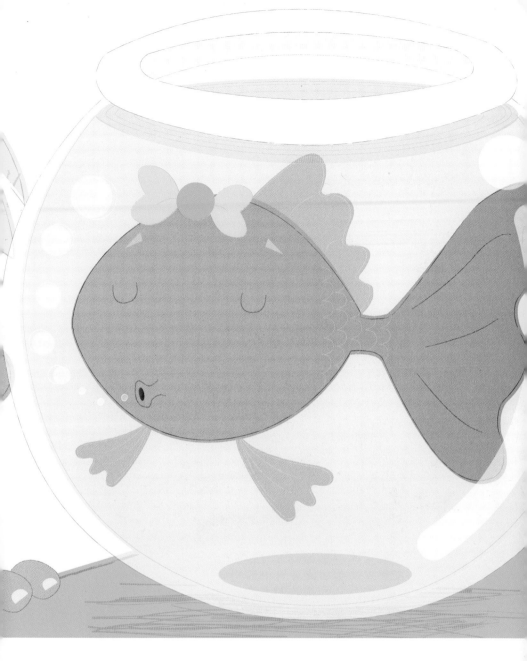

Nibbles blows bubbles.

"You're right. We better get busy," Andy says.

Andy pulls everything out of his dresser and closet.

Nothing seems right.

Andy checks his craft box. He
finds paper, glue, and scissors.

"This brown paper might work.
We can be lions," Andy says.

Nibbles does not look happy.

"You're right. It will be perfect
for me, but we can't put paper in
water for you," Andy says.

Nibbles moves her tail faster
and faster.

"Don't worry, Nibbles," Andy says. "I'll think of something."

Andy thinks of another idea.

"We'll be spiders. I can glue
four legs on each side of you,"
he says.

Nibbles does not look happy.

"That's right. You don't like
spiders," says Andy. "What am
I going to do?"

Andy sits at his desk. He watches Nibbles swim.

"I've got it! I have to get busy,"
Andy says.

Andy cuts, glues, and stuffs all afternoon.

"This will be the best party
ever!" Andy says.

Later that day, the doorbell rings.
It's the Pet Club.

They are all dressed up. Their
pets are dressed up, too.

"Sharks!" Kayla and Lucy yell.

"Cool," Jake says.

"Thanks," Andy says.

Nibbles finally looks happy.

STORY WORDS

Halloween   costume   bubbles

closet   craft   scissors

spiders   sharks

Total Word Count: 282

Join the Pet Club today!